Sarah the Spider and the Barn Dancers

Hilary Robinson · Illustration Jane Abbott

Sarah the Spider had opened a school –
Pinned to the door was a very firm rule,
That for spectacular shows pupils must wear
Beautiful costumes and bands in their hair.

Barney Owl read it and called out aloud,
'This rule must be kept,' he said to the crowd.
'Now let me present Dame Sarah our own –
The best ballet teacher the world's ever known.'

To wild applause Sarah curtseyed and bowed
Positioned herself and then said, 'I'm proud
To announce to you all an important date
There's only one week to the annual fete.'

'I have been asked by the fete's organizer
To put on a show and be dance supervisor.
We're all going to learn a wonderful treat,
The amazing, the classical, Nutcracker Suite.'

'A word if you please,' said Percy the Pig,
'I don't have hair and I don't have a wig.
A hair band on me wouldn't look right
Wrapped round my head I would look quite a sight.'

'Excuse us a minute,' bleated the sheep,
'We produce wool, heap upon heap.
We're sure that between us a wig could be made
Tied to his head and pinned up with braid.'

Percy had always cherished a dream
To be a star dancer as Sarah had been.
But pigs like Percy are often quite shy
Preferring to practise alone in their sty.

'Barney,' said Sarah, 'and I are agreed
That Percy the Pig should take on the lead.
Attend please each day, here in this dairy,
To learn the steps of the Sugar Plum Fairy.'

Percy fell to the floor, fainting from shock,
Mother Hen flew to him bringing her flock.
They fluttered their wings to keep him awake
He jumped to his feet and started to shake.

'I can't believe this, I am so excited,
To take on the lead of course I'm delighted.
The Sugar Plum Fairy, my dream has come true!
Thank you, dear Sarah, and thanks Barney, too.'

Next day in the dairy the friends all filed in,
They stood in a line keen to begin.
'Right,' called Sarah, tapping her stick,
'Step to the right, then point, bend and kick!'

Day after day they worked on their drills,
Dancing routines and theatrical skills.
At the end of each session Sarah gave tips
About tying up hair with ribbons and clips.

And even at night Percy worked hard,
While his friends were asleep he'd go into the yard
Perfecting each move by the light of the moon
As he sang to himself the Nutcracker tune.

The day of the fete at last came around.
Farmyards of animals flocked to the grounds.
Back at the school Sarah calmed all the worries
Of nervous barn dancers in all kinds of flurries.

There were stalls for jams and cakes and sweets,
A tombola, a raffle, lucky dips full of treats.
The Carnival Queen wore a long velvet gown,
Her head adorned with a glorious crown.

And when that was done it was time for the show,
'Right,' called Barney, 'are we ready to go?'
Dressed up in their costumes they arrived on a cart
Then jumped on the stage ready to start.

As the music began Percy started to cry.
'What's the matter?' asked Sarah. 'You feeling shy?'
'No,' Percy said, his face turning red,
'Everyone's mocking the wig on my head.'

He stared straight ahead, unable to move,
Tears rolled down his cheeks, how could he prove
That he was a dancer, not a pig looking scary,
But a pig that could dance like the Sugar Plum Fairy?

The show must go on so they all danced around
As Percy stood there, feet fixed to the ground.
'Come on,' they whispered, 'give it a go.
You know you can do it...point that big toe!'

Percy summoned up courage and wiggled his hips,
Moved round the stage with a series of skips.
He leapt to the centre, spun round on the spot,
Now was the time to give all he'd got.

The audience hushed, amazed by his skill,
A pig who could dance was quite a big thrill.
Sarah's school had given Percy the chance
To prove that he had a future in dance.

At the end of the show the audience cheered
As up on the stage Sarah appeared.
'Thank you,' she said, 'but just one more thing,
I want to crown Percy the Carnival King!'

For Charlotte, who'd love to see Piglet jiglet, with love HR
For Damien, with love, JA

First published in the UK in 1999 by
Belitha Press Limited, London House, Great Eastern Wharf,
Parkgate Road, London SW11 4NQ.

ISBN 1 84138 101 2 (hardback)
ISBN 1 84138 045 8 (paperback)

British Library Cataloguing in Publication Data for this
book is available from the British Library

Printed in Hong Kong

Editor: Honor Head
Designer: Simeen Karim